COOKIE & Milk

A SCIENTIFICALLY STUNT-TASTIC SISTERHOOD

BY MICHELE MCAVOY

ILLUSTRATED BY JESSICA GIBSON

COOKIE & Milk
A SCIENTIFICALLY STUNT-TASTIC SISTERHOOD

Printed in China and published by Cardinal Rule Press.
Visit us at www.CardinalRulePress.com

Summary: A story of friendship that transcends stereotypes. Cookie and Milk shows young readers that it may not be what you have in common that sparks a true friendship but how you differ.

Our books may be purchased in bulk for promotional, educational or business use. Please contact your local bookseller or IPC Books at orders@ipgbook.com

Library of Congress Control Number: 2018959430
ISBN (hardcover) 978-0-9976085-8-8
ISBN (picture book) 978-0-9976085-9-5

The art in this book was created using Adobe Photoshop and a Wacom Cintiq
Book design by Emily Love O'Malley

Cardinal Rule Press
5449 Sylvia
Dearborn, MI 48125
VISIT US AT WWW.CARDINALRULEPRESS.COM

BEFORE READING

* Read the title of the book. Ask your child if they like cookies and milk. Does a cookie taste better when had alongside a glass of milk?

* This book is about diversity in friendship. Have your child name a friend. How is their friend different from them? In what ways is that friend the same as them?

DURING READING

* This book is about how different character traits can complement each other.

* Point out examples of how the characters Cookie & Milk are different both physically and personality-wise from each other.

* Encourage your child to share which character they relate to more, Cookie or Milk, and why?

* Discuss what "opposites attract" means and how no two people are exactly the same.

AFTER READING

* This book is also about diversity in families.

* Explain how Cookie & Milk could look different from each other and be sisters.

* Define blended families to your child (step-sisters and step-brothers.)

* Talk about multi-racial families (how children can inherit different traits from their parents.)

* This is a great opportunity to discuss adoption.

* Read the "Did You Know" section at the back of the book.

* Talk about how girls are adventurous and are scientists, astronauts and doctors, just like boys.

* Encourage your child to appreciate and respect the differences in their friends and their peers. Teach your child to be themselves and strive to achieve what makes them happy, whether enjoying science and math or being athletic and adventurous– or a little bit of everything! Remind your child that he or she can do whatever they put their mind to.

For my Dear Friend, Wose.
Our friendship has always
been like a sisterhood.

M.M.

To my loving family. Especially
my mother, who believed in my
artistic talent and motivated me
to pursue my career.

J.G.

Once upon a time, there were two little girls who were nothing alike.

Hi. I am Cookie.

My real name is Khloe, but my dad calls me Cookie because he says I'm sweet.

And they call me Milk. Not because my skin is really white, which it is, but because my little brother can't say Mikaela, which is my real name. So, they call me Milk.

I like it though, because it reminds me of my little brother, and that's cool.

I'm not as smart as Cookie. But, what I lack in the science and math department I make up for in the adventure department.

Milk's favorite words start with "S"– Sports, Stunts and Stitches.

and sneakers, and soccer, and surfing. You get the point. Cookie's favorite "S" words are science, sigma (it's a math term, don't ask) and space, like outer–space.

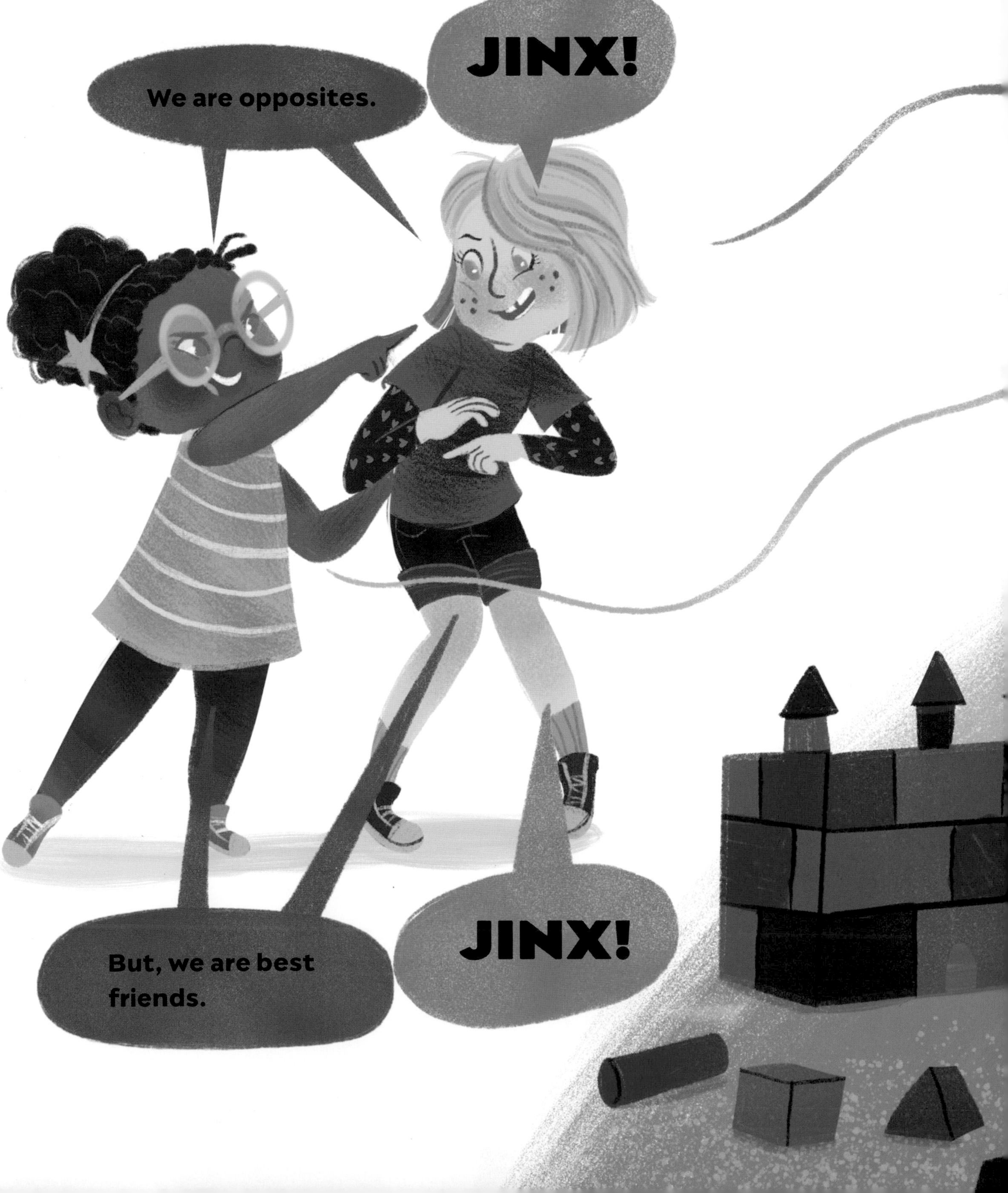
We are opposites.
JINX!
But, we are best friends.
JINX!

If only you saw Milk surf that enormous wave. It was pure magic.

I have Cookie to thank for that. She studied the tides, the moon and the wind to make sure I caught the most tubular-tastic ride.

See, when we were little we didn't realize that smart and sporty could go together.

But, I truly couldn’t be me without Cookie.
And I couldn’t be me without Milk.
JINX!
Doesn’t count.

Could two little girls who look nothing alike...and act nothing alike...be best friends?

DID YOU KNOW?

Astronaut: Valentina Tereshkova was the first woman to go into space. She orbited Earth 48 times!

Doctor: Elizabeth Blackwell was America's first female doctor. She had to be voted into college!

Mathematician: Katherine Johnson, Mary Jackson, and Dorothy Vaughan are three famous female mathematicians who worked for the space program at NASA. They were considered human computers!

Programmer: Ada Lovelace was the first woman computer programmer. Her nickname was The Enchantress of Numbers!

Engineer, doctor, and astronaut: Mae Carol Jemison was the first African-American woman to travel in space. She was an astronaut, an engineer, and a doctor! She spent 190 hours, 30 minutes, and 23 seconds in space!

Explorer: Junko Tabei was the first woman to climb Mount Everest. Mount Everest is Earth's highest mountain!

Skateboarder: Patti McGee was the first woman to be inducted into the Skateboarding Hall of Fame. Her first skateboard was built by her brother from her own roller skates!

Surfer: Margo Oberg is considered the first professional female surfer. She surfed her first wave at age 10!

Pilot: Amelia Mary Earhart was the first woman pilot to fly across the Atlantic Ocean all by herself!

"S" WORDS THAT MAKE A BEST FRIEND

Smile
Someone that makes you smile & laugh . . . often.

Secret
Someone who will keep your secret no matter how juicy.

Support
Someone who will cheer you on even when they are competing in the same event.

Steady
Someone who does not flip flop their friendship. They are always there for you.

Safe
Someone who makes you feel safe to be 100% yourself.

Michele McAvoy is an award-winning children's book author from New Jersey. As a child, she read Judy Blume and drew Garfield comics. For her 10th birthday, she asked for a pink typewriter. Michele always loved the smell of new books. Now all grown up (typewriters near obsolete) she loves bringing joy to children through her own stories.

Jessica Gibson is a self-taught professional illustrator based in Michigan who has been illustrating for children's publishing since 2016. Besides picture books, her artwork has been featured in publications such as "American Girl Magazine."